Good Night, Forest

Written by Denise Brennan-Nelson

Illustrated by Marco Bucci

Good morning, forest.
Rise and shine!
Good morning, maple,
Oak, and pine.

Good morning, sun!
Hello, day!
Good morning, deer.
Want to play?

Good morning, bird.
Sing your song.

Good morning, stream.
Hum along.

Good morning, chipmunk,
Squirrel, too.

Good morning, beaver.
There's work to do.

Good morning, flowers
        And rustling leaves.
Good morning, cricket
        And gentle breeze.

Hello, porcupine,
You look lively!
Good day, moss,
Ferns, and ivy.

Hello, turtle.
Come out of your shell.

Good day, skunk.
What's that smell?

Deep in the forest,
The creatures play,

But something happens
At the end of the day.

A hush falls over,
Wide and deep;
Even the forest
Has to sleep.

Good night, trees.
Good night, stream.
Good night, otter.
Time to dream.

Good night, critters.
Good night, day.
Sleepy time.
No more play.

Good night, bird.
Find your nest.
Good night, forest.
Get some rest.

Good night, ant.
Where's your hill?

Good night, bunny.
Soft and still.

Good night, bear.
No more growl.
Good night, coyote.
Quiet howl.

Time to sleep!
All creatures do.
Good night, forest.
Good night, you.

For Kiera, Breslin, Harper and Lena

—Denise

★

For the Bucci canoeing crew.

—Marco

Sleeping Bear Press
2395 South Huron Parkway, Suite 200
Ann Arbor, MI 48104
www.sleepingbearpress.com

Printed and bound in the United States.

10 9 8 7 6 5 4 3 2 1

Library of Congress Cataloging-in-Publication Data

Names: Brennan-Nelson, Denise, author. | Bucci, Marco, illustrator.
Title: Good night, Forest / written by Denise Brennan-Nelson ;
illustrated by Marco Bucci.
Description: Ann Arbor, MI : Sleeping Bear Press, [2018] | Summary:
Illustrations and simple text provide a greeting to Forest's plants,
animals, sunshine, and waters, then bids them all good night.
Identifiers: LCCN 2017029874 | ISBN 9781585363889
Subjects: | CYAC: Stories in rhyme. | Forests and forestry—Fiction. |
Forest animals—Fiction. | Bedtime—Fiction.
Classification: LCC PZ8.3.B7457 Gm 2018 | DDC [E]—dc23
LC record available at https://lccn.loc.gov/2017029874